The Princess
Who Wore Glasses

Written by

Laura Hertzfeld Katz

Illustrated by **Jacob Duncan**

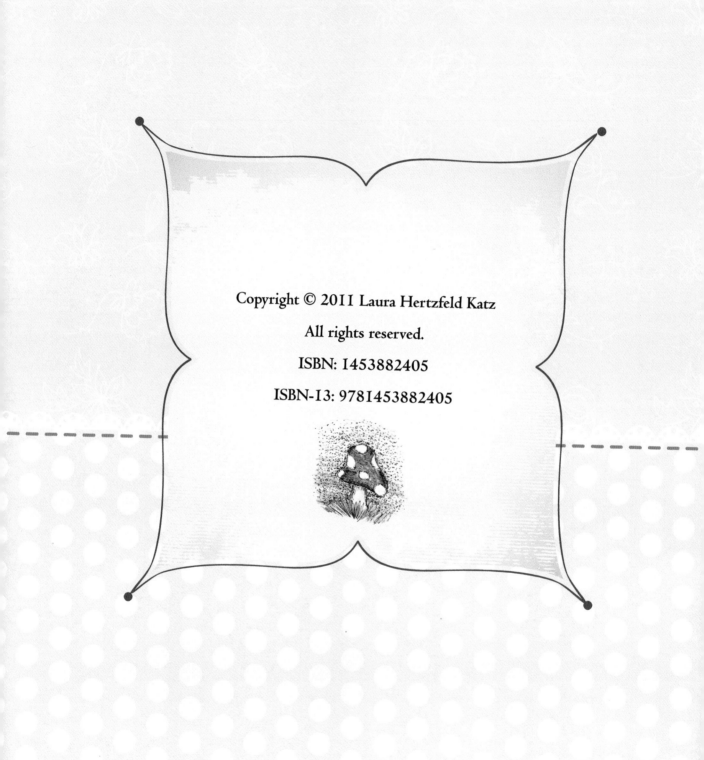

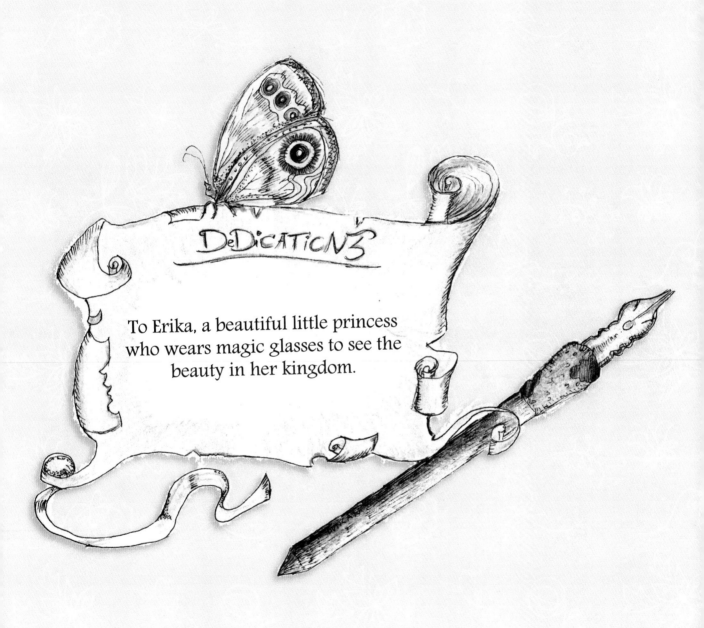

DeDicATioNS

To Erika, a beautiful little princess who wears magic glasses to see the beauty in her kingdom.

nce upon a time, there was a kingdom named
TuaLuna. All around TuaLuna were beautiful flowers,
majestic willow trees, and colorful birds.

$\mathcal{I}$n the kingdom lived a princess named Liana, who had bright blue eyes, golden hair, and a very happy heart. Princess Liana loved to look out through her bedroom window at all the wonders of the kingdom.

But she had a secret:

She could not see everything clearly; some things were blurry.

O ne day after school as the princess twirled and danced in the meadow, she heard music in the willow trees. "Mommy," asked Liana, "why are the trees singing?"

"Don't you see the beautiful red, yellow and blue birds singing their happy songs up in the trees, Liana?" asked Queen Victoria.

"No, Mommy. Where? I want to see them!" the princess exclaimed.

That night the queen explained to King Edward, "Liana cannot see things that are far away from her. Today she danced to the songs of the birds in the willows, but she couldn't see them."

The king was quite curious, and asked, "Liana, will you take a walk with me to the balcony?"

"Sure Daddy," replied the princess.

*A*s they stood under the magnificent night sky, the king asked, "Liana, what shape is our moon tonight?"

"Um … a circle? I'm not sure, Daddy. Is that it over there…?" The king realized that his little girl could not clearly see the moon and stars.

"Liana," asked the king, "how would you like to see the moon better?"

Liana beamed. "Oh, Daddy, can that happen? And all the birds too?"

"Yes, sweetheart, and all the birds too," promised the king.

As the king and queen discussed Liana's eyesight, they decided that Liana should visit the court magician, Maximilian. The king said, "He will know exactly what to do! I shall take Liana to see him tomorrow!" The queen agreed that this was an excellent plan.

ith great anticipation, the king and princess left early the next morning in the royal carriage for the village where Maximilian lived. Liana asked, "Daddy, will I be able to see butterflies too?"

"Yes, Liana, and ladybugs, too!" the king said.

"Are we there yet? Are we there yet?" the princess asked eagerly.

"Almost, Princess," he chuckled.

$\mathcal{M}$aximilian was only too happy to help the king with his request, and invited them into his workshop. "Welcome, Princess Liana."

*M*aximilian asked Liana to sit in the magic seeing chair. Then he said gently, "Look into the big kaleidoscope and tell me what you see."

"I see beautiful red hearts, and they're getting bigger! I see bright and shiny yellow stars! And swirls! Everything is so clear! It really *is* magic!" she exclaimed.

"Why yes, it's eye magic!" said the magician. "Soon you will see all things near and far." Princess Liana jumped off the chair and giggle-squealed with joy.

*M*aximilian left the room to work his magic and soon returned to present Princess Liana with the most beautiful pair of eyeglasses she could imagine. They had swirls of purple, pink, and blue to match her eyes. Her name was even etched in gold on them!

$\mathcal{T}$he princess put on the glasses and jumped up and down in amazement. She flapped her arms with delight, shouting, "I can see! I can see! I can see so many new things!" For Liana, it was like being in a whole new world!

*A*s they were leaving, Princess Liana thanked the magician, then, asked the king, "Daddy, may we go to the singing trees? I want to see the birds that sing their happy songs! Please?"

When they arrived at the willow trees, the princess laughed with joy. "Daddy, now I can really see them! I see yellow birds and red birds! Wow, there's a blue bird way up high, singing to her babies!"

𝒯hen Princess Liana saw the most amazing thing of all. She noticed that the meadow was filled with tiny yellow flowers. "Daddy, look! What are these?"

"Those my little princess are buttercups. I planted them here when you were born, because they matched the color of your hair. And we wanted the whole kingdom to know our joy of having you."

"They are so lovely, Daddy! Thank you," Liana said.

*L*ater, Princess Liana was excited to see the night sky with her glasses on. "I see the man in the moon! And the stars are twinkling at me! Daddy, nighttime is so beautiful!"

The king smiled happily as he watched his daughter's excitement.

At bedtime, Liana told the queen everything about her awesome day. Then she asked, "Mommy, may I wear my new glasses to sleep? I want my dreams to be magical too."

"Well, okay, perhaps for a little while," the queen said with a smile.

The next day, Princess Liana couldn't wait to show her eyeglasses to her friends at school. "What are *those*?" they asked.

"These are my magic glasses. I can see *everything* when I wear them," the princess replied. Then she opened her eyes extra wide and said, "Oh, Erika, what beautiful stars in your hair! Lizzie, you have strawberries on your dress; they look yummy! Sarah, you have beautiful green eyes. You are so pretty!"

"What about me? What about me?" her other friends asked. They all wanted to know the new things Liana could see about them.

"I see everything!" she exclaimed. "I see your bows, your smiles, your ribbons, and your lace!" With that, Liana's friends knew that her glasses were truly magic.

A nd that is the story of how the beautiful Princess Liana of TuaLuna came to wear glasses.

Questions from Princess Liana

Are you a princess who wears magic glasses?

I was so excited to get my glasses that I jumped for joy and giggle-squealed. Can you giggle-squeal?

What color glasses did you get? Are you excited?

What can you see now about your friends that you couldn't see before?

Did you show your new eyeglasses to your friends and family? Who?

What can you see now in your kingdom that you didn't notice before?

What can you do now, with glasses, that you could not do before?

Did you know that wearing eyeglasses is a gift, too? It has been one of my favorites.

Hints for Parents:

Sometimes as parents, we don't realize that young children can have vision problems. If you notice that your child often gets headaches, or says that her eyes are tired; if she has difficulty identifying things, trips over items, or sits very close to the television or computer, it might be time to get her eyes checked. Today, your pediatrician may be able to check your child's eyes during an office visit. But this exam may not catch everything. Trust your instincts. If you still think there is a problem, make an appointment at a family eye care center to have your child's eyes examined.

Get excited for your child's first visit to an eye care center. She will be more comfortable about the idea of glasses if you are!

Allow your child to pick out her own glasses! If she loves the way they look and feel, she will wear them. Pink, purple, green, blue; swirls or dots; round, oval, or rectangle … they're all fashionable and fun!

Be your child's best cheerleader. Praise her for making the good choice of wearing her magical glasses when needed and taking good care of them.

About the Author

Laura Hertzfeld Katz is a licensed marriage and family therapist. She currently lives in Cary, North Carolina with her family. She wears pink eyeglasses with purple swirls. Of this book, the author says, "My friend's daughter was the inspiration for this book. When she learned she had to wear glasses she exclaimed, 'but Mommy, there are no princesses who wear glasses!'

As parents, we know that if children think they are in some way different from their peers, it could make them feel anxious and insecure. We must help our children see that it is these differences that make them fully who they are- make them perfectly themselves! I invite you to turn getting eyeglasses into a wonderful, magical journey for your child."

About the Illustrator

Jacob Duncan is a young illustrator who lives on a farm in Holly Springs, North Carolina. In his first full-length children's book, Jacob brings Princess Liana and the kingdom of TuaLuna to life in the hearts of little princesses around the world.

Acknowledgements:

Thank you to: Matthew Szymanski, Derek Leek, Sarah Tilton, Shuroma Herekar, and Dave Katz for all of your expertise and support in making this story come alive in the hearts of little girls.

Made in the USA
Lexington, KY
29 April 2014